For my son, David,
with love and appreciation
—N.L.

For Martin and Harry
—T.T.D.

Published by Peter Pauper Press, Inc.
202 Mamaroneck Avenue
White Plains, New York 10601 USA

Library of Congress Control Number: 2019951509

ISBN 978-1-4413-3264-6

Manufactured for Peter Pauper Press, Inc.
Printed in Hong Kong

7 6 5 4 3 2 1

Visit us at www.peterpauper.com

HOW I TRAINED MY DOG IN 10 DAYS

By
Norma Lewis

Illustrated by
Tom Tinn-Disbury

PETER PAUPER PRESS, INC.
White Plains, New York

I don't want to brag, but it only took me ten days to train my dog Scamp.

Here's how I did it.

Day 1

Okay, Scamp, this is how
it's going to be.
Here is your doghouse where
you will sleep.

You may go into the backyard,
but you *have* to stay out of the flower bed,
and you absolutely cannot go
into the house.

Day 2

Scamp, listen up.
Alright, you may go into the backyard and even help in
the garden. I'll let you come into the family room, but
you are *not* allowed to play my video games.

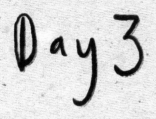

Day 3

Scamp, it's like this.

You may go into the backyard, and the family room.

You are allowed to help with the garden, and, *okay*, . . . you can play my video games. But . . .

you definitely have to keep out of the dining room.

Day 4

Scamp! Please pay attention.

You may go into the backyard, the family room, *and* the dining room.

You are allowed to help with the garden, and play my video games, but . . . you are NOT allowed to eat at the dining room table.

Day 5

Okay, Scamp, here's the drill.
I typed up the list.

**Scamp is permitted
to go into the:**

- Backyard
- Family Room
- ~~Dinig~~ Dining Room

He is aLLowed to:

- Help with the Garden
- Play Video games
- eat at the ~~dinig~~ Dining
  room table

?

Day 6

Okay, I'm in charge here, Scamp.
Let's review the list.

Scamp is permitted
to go into the:

· Backyard
· Family Room
· ~~Dinig~~ Dining Room

· Bathroom

He is allowed to:

· Help with the Garden
· Play Video games
· eat at the ~~dinig~~ Dining
  room table

Now, Scamp, listen closely.
You are one-hundred percent not allowed
to take a bubble bath.

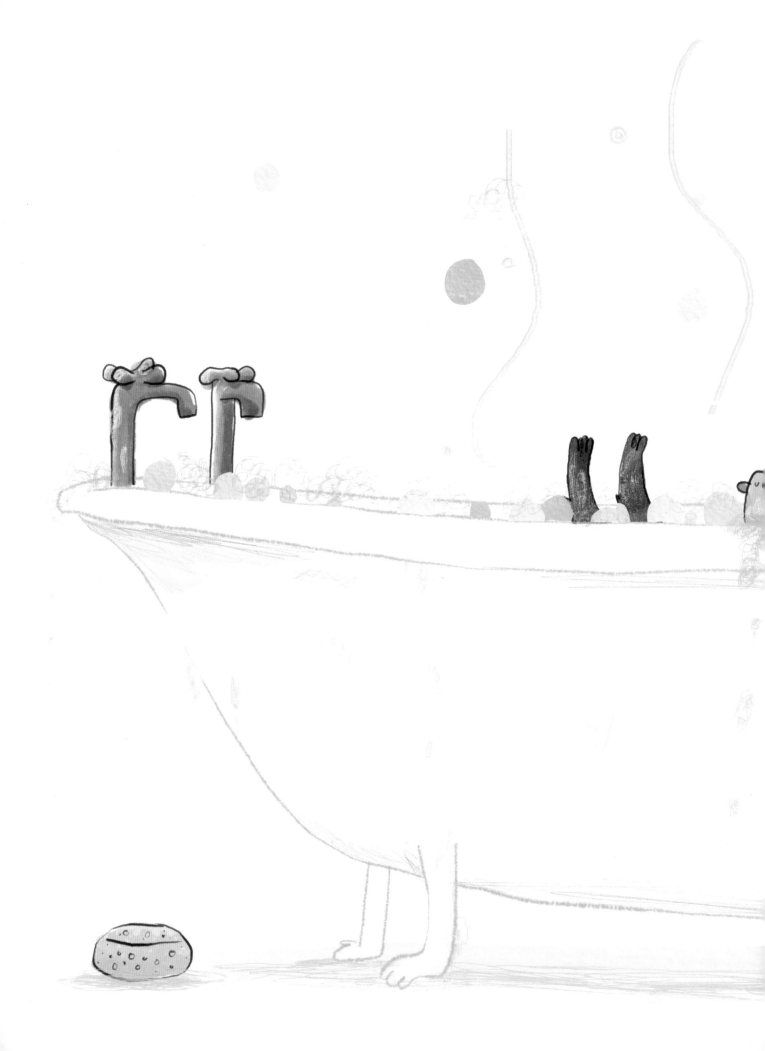

Day 7

Scamp!
Okay, new plan.
Here's the final list.

Scamp is permitted to go into the:

- Backyard
- Family Room
- ~~Dinig~~ Dining Room
  - Bathroom

He is aLLowed to:

- Help with the Garden
- Play Video games
- eat at the ~~dinig~~ Dining room table
  - Take a Bubble bath

Scamp, now I'm being serious.
You are absolutely,
positively,

NOT
permitted in my room.

Day 8

Scamp! We're going to review the revised
and FINAL list
one
more
time.

Scamp is permitted to go into the:

- Backyard
- Family Room
- ~~Dinig~~ Dining Room
- Bathroom
- My room

He is aLLowed to:

- Help with the Garden
- Play Video games
- eat at the ~~dinig~~ Dining room table
- Take a Bubble bath

One last thing. Are you listening, Scamp?
Do not even *think* about sleeping on my bed.

Day 9

Okay, Scamp, let's get this straight.
You may go into the backyard, the family room, the
dining room, the bathroom, and even my room.

You are allowed to help with the garden, play my video games,
eat at the dining room table, take a bubble bath,
and I'll let you sleep on my bed.

But . . . the pillow . . . is
MINE!
Understood?

Day 10

Scamp, move your head over. Okay?
Scamp? Please?

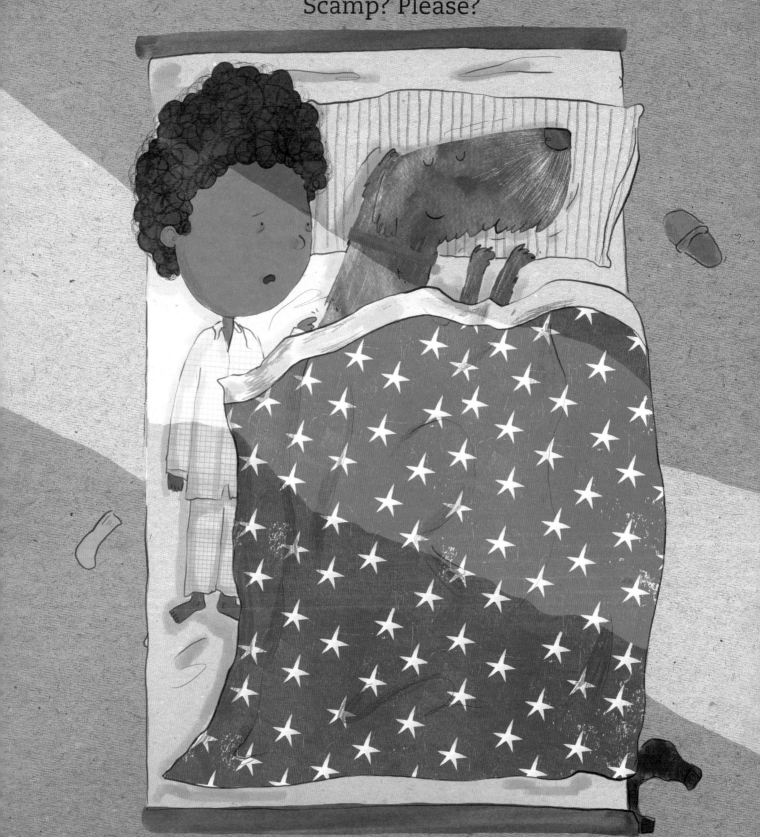

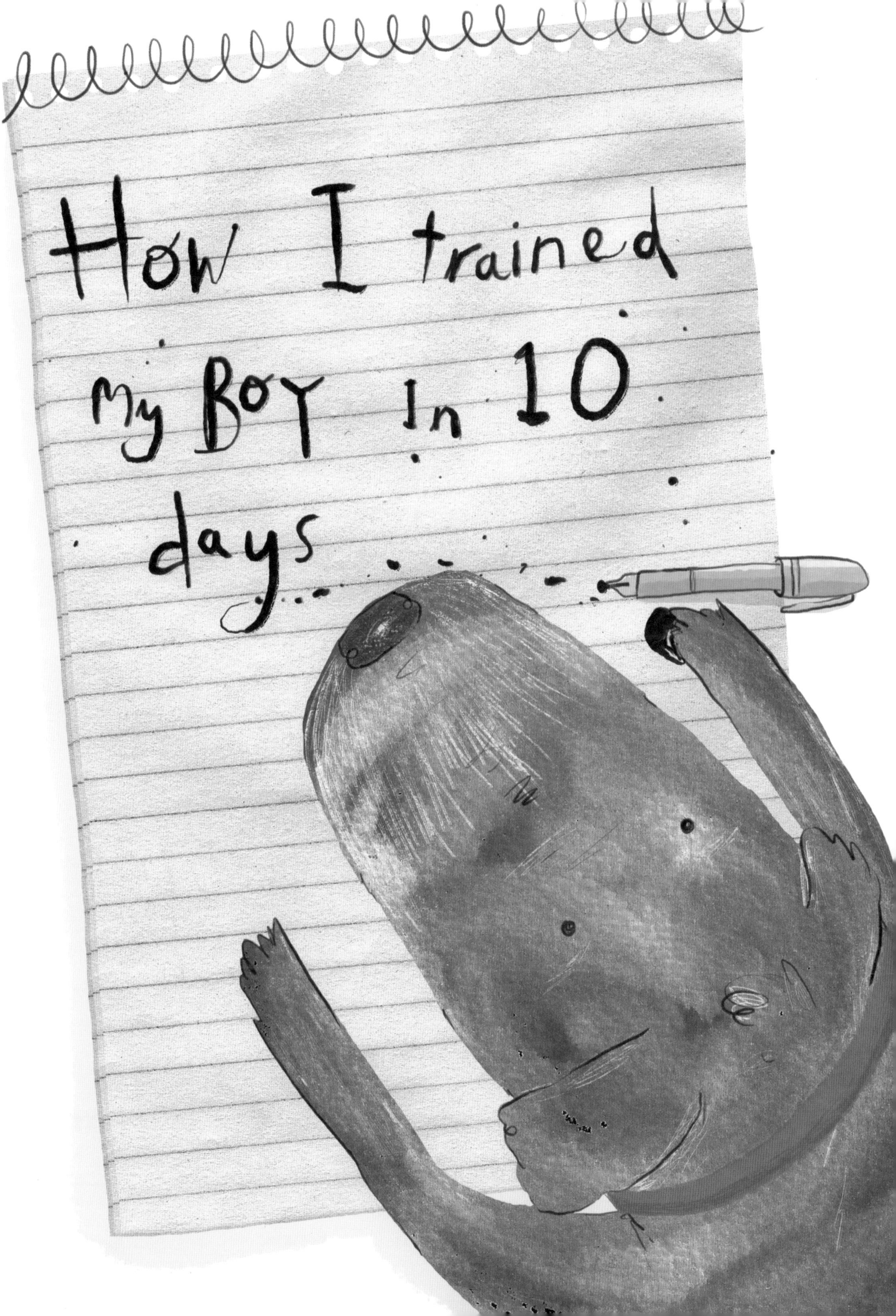
How I trained
my BOY In 10
days